I0712750

The Bedtime Story of Falling Rock

The Bedtime Story of
Falling Rock

A Tale of True Love

Story by Justin Kerson

Illustrations by Eloy Bida

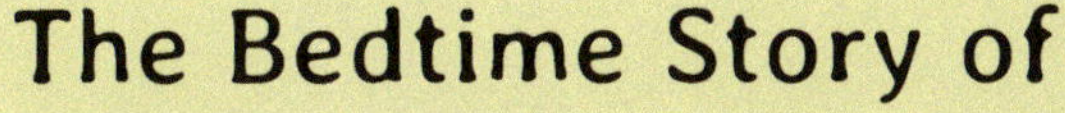

The Bedtime Story of Falling Rock is a fictional story based on nonfictional characters and events. Set between 1801 and 1845, the tale takes place in a valley sheltered from the Pacific Ocean by Mount Tamalpais, in the terrain today we know as West Marin.

ISBN   979-8-9886011-0-4 (hard cover)
        979-8-9886011-1-1 (ePub)

Illustrations and cover art by Eloy Bida
Book design by Paul Nylander | Illustrada

Set in Averia Libre and Raleway

Published by ToTTGlobal in San Francisco, 2023
ToTTGlobal.com

To Dad,
Brazil,
And every lover
lost along the way
in finding myself
where I am today.

Aho Mitakuye Oyasin

Lakota prayer of
oneness and harmony
with all relations,
in all forms of life—
animals,
people,
bugs,
birds,
trees,
and even rocks,
rivers,
mountains
and valleys
on this great earth
and beyond.

Prologue

Falling Rock and Tamalpais is a twining tale of two lovers
whose souls skipped together amongst many lives.
This is the story of just one of their lives.

In 1818, in the foothills of present-day Marin County, lived a tribe of Native Americans called the **Miwok**. They were peaceful hunter-gatherers who had many villages in the land stretching from Sonoma County to San Francisco. With their handmade canoes, they were able to navigate the Northern California coast from what is now known as **Tomales Bay.**

The land offered beauty and an abundance of resources—redwood bark for shelter, shells for bartering, obsidian for jewelry and tools, and grasses for baskets. Berries and flowers furnished food and dyes. There were also roots, herbs, minerals, and hemp to be used medicinally and in **peace pipe ceremonies**. Acorns, fish, and deer provided nourishment. The Miwok had a vast knowledge of their plentiful environment, utilizing and protecting its natural wealth.

Let it be known that the Miwok, although peaceful, were very competitive by nature and loved all kinds of games, including guessing games, dice games, and archery. Competition was a healthy part of the community. One of their wisest, most honorable elders, Chief Marin—who bequeathed his name to Marin County— also loved a good challenge.

Chief Marin's daughter, Tamalpais, was the princess of this mystic land and a child-hood friend of Falling Rock. The two were born the same year and grew up together. Falling Rock was raised by his mother and his grandfather, Stalking Wolf. His father, Ewok, was set to be the next chief of the Miwok, but while out hunting with his best friend Marin, he perished, and that is how Tam's father became the chief.

Tamalpais was raised by her father, Chief Marin, just north of **The Good Eye of the Turtle** (how this spot got its name, The Good Eye of the Turtle, is its own little story…). Tam's mother had passed while she was an infant, but she had a lovely, happy childhood, although now and then her asthma flared up, which was always worse in the spring. Living in the geographic region of the Good Eye of the Turtle, which received the freshest air pouring in from the Pacific Ocean, helped tremendously, but Marin still kept a watchful eye over Tam's health.

Season after season, Tam and Falling Rock would swim, laugh, and explore their beautiful land. As they grew, so did their friendship, and by the time Tam and Falling Rock were about sixteen, their bodies were starting to change and their feelings for one another developed. Butterflies fluttered in their stomachs when they came close to one another. The two childhood friends fell in love.

Just like the blooming love between Tam and Falling Rock, beautiful flowers began to show their colors across the land with the coming of spring. The Miwok were happy to see the flowers bloom, because the previous year had been **The Year Without A Summer,** when winter had lasted all year long. But this year was different—the flowers bloomed bigger than they ever had before. With more flowers, of course, comes more pollen. In fact, so many storms hit the coast at this time that they caused a pollen bloom unlike any spring the Miwok had ever seen. Even the elders could not remember a spring filled with so many storms.

After ten days of lightning, thunder, and hail, the Chief was very worried about Tam's asthma. She was beginning to have severe attacks, and the **Yerba Buena** tea that usually healed her lungs was no longer helping. The medicine woman of the village told the Chief that he needed to forage for a very specific herb to help his daughter.

Unable to leave his vulnerable tribe to search for the herb himself, the Chief declared a contest to help Tam. He invited all the great warriors, and great men in general, to participate in a competitive quest for medicinal herbs. The prize would be his daughter's hand in marriage! Tam's father only wanted the best for his precious girl. He did not take Falling Rock seriously as a suitor. He only saw Falling Rock as a boy and a childhood friend to Tam, not as a man worthy of being his daughter's mate.

Chief Marin's attitude was very worrisome for Falling Rock and Tam, but there was little they could do. In those times, men and women did not marry a partner of the same age. A woman married an older man who could offer her family some sort of material and social benefit, or at least prove that he was able to provide for her and their future family. In this case, the partner of Tamalpais was to become the next Miwok chief. Many of the villagers did not believe that Falling Rock was ready for such a lofty position. Chief Marin could not bear to look at or be around Falling Rock because it reminded him of the pain he felt over losing his best friend, Ewok.

Falling Rock's hunting ability was unrecognized in the village. Even though Falling Rock was only sixteen, he was skilled in stalking and tracking. He had picked up hunting skills from his grandfather, Stalking Wolf, before he had entered the spirit world. Stalking Wolf had taught Falling Rock from a young age to hide his strength, because he knew that if your enemy does not know your strength, you can always surprise him. But Tam knew that Falling Rock was just as strong and wise as the very best men because of all the time they had spent together in the wild.

Falling Rock was as worried as Chief Marin about Tam's health when the Ten Days of Storms came to the land. Falling Rock was never far from her side. One day, he overheard the shaman talking of the sacred herb that would make Tam better, something called the **Elecampane Root**, which the Miwok also knew as Horse-Heel. It grew inland, a few days' worth of travel away, in a place that was called the **Lake in the Sky** (Lake Tahoe). The root was to be found at the bottom of the pool into which the **Emerald Falls** flowed.

Chief Marin held a meeting in the big sweat lodge. Since Tam was beautiful, kind, funny, and the chief's daughter, all the great warriors and noblemen showed up at the meeting to learn more about the contest. Falling Rock was the **fire stoker.** As the meeting commenced, he couldn't help but overhear the details while he carried the smoldering rocks on two deer antlers back and forth from the fire to the lodge. The hot rocks steamed and hissed as raindrops from the damp night fell upon them.

Once all the visitors had settled into the **sweat lodge,** the chief began to speak about the Elecampane Root. This hard-to-find herb only grew in the Emerald Falls that poured into the Lake in the Sky, far away from the village of **Huimen** (modern day West Marin). The rules of the contest were as follows: whoever managed to get the Miwok shaman the root needed to save Tam's life would have his daughter's hand in marriage. This was no easy task. It would take at least two weeks to get to Emerald Falls and back.

Falling Rock put the last stone on the fire in the sweat lodge and took his place in the back row of tribesmen. Falling Rock watched as an elder folded the blanket over the door for the start of the cleansing ceremony. The men chanted and sweated through the peak of the night's darkness. Songs were sung and pipes were passed from great hunter to honorable elder to boat maker, back to another hunter, and so on.

In the midst of these rituals, Falling Rock had a vision of himself in the future coming upon the Great Lake in the Sky and standing upon the waterfall. He slipped, fell, and plunged into the water beneath the falls. When he surfaced, his breath had the air that was needed to save Tam's life. Coming out of his trance, Falling Rock was met by the knowing gaze of the shaman, as if they had shared the same vision. With dawn on its way, the stones in the middle of the sweat lodge began to cool and the chief ended the ceremony. The men exited the sweat lodge in the proper clockwise fashion, for this was tradition.

After the sweat lodge ceremony, Falling Rock went to Tam's bedside to see how she was doing. Her throat was swollen and her eyes were watering. She was sick, fading, and talking about herself in the third person with premonitions of what was to come. He kissed Tam goodbye and told her that he would return with the root for her medicine. He took off at dawn behind all the other men who had already left for the Lake in the Sky.

As the golden hour of morning came, others in the village noticed that Falling Rock was nowhere to be seen. The Miwok knew then that he had set out on his own quest to save Tam's life, unbound by the rules that Chief Marin had laid down for the other men.

The journey to the Emerald Falls was not an easy one. All the competitors and Falling Rock crossed the mountains, sweating through the hot days and shivering through the cold, crisp spring nights. They crossed deserts on the long journey, the only river along the way still frozen in some sections, and the mountain pass still covered with snow.

The Lake in the Sky was inhabited by a not-so-peaceful, more rugged tribe, the **Paiutes**, who were known to capture and enslave men passing through their territory. Giving them up as sacrificial offerings to the legendary cannibal Red-head **Nephilim** Giants, of **Lovelock**. But that's another tale. The Miwok were happy to live a great distance from these people, and the land of the legendary giants, but by avoiding contact and trade altogether, the necessary herbs were even harder to obtain.

Falling Rock traveled quickly through the rough terrain. He was not concerned with earning Tam's hand in marriage—the only thing that kept him moving was saving her life. It had been about a week now since he and the other men left Huimen, and now he was only hours away from the Emerald Falls. Unfortunately this meant he had entered the land of the Paiutes. Since he had spent so much time hunting and stalking animals in the hills surrounding his village, Falling Rock knew how to move stealthily through Paiute territory.

As he was walking along the tree line up high in the hills, he noticed a Paiute camp down in the valley. He could see Chief Marin's best friend **Edward S. Curtis** and **Sub-Chief Quentin** had been captured and were tied up behind the main camp. He thought to himself that they must have been caught because they were so eager to get to the Emerald Falls that they had forgotten to move quietly and carefully to avoid the Paiute. Falling Rock knew that neither man thought very much of him—they always cast him aside, judging him too young or too slow to partake of the hunts, but Falling Rock could not let anything happen to them. Not helping these men would only hurt his own tribe.

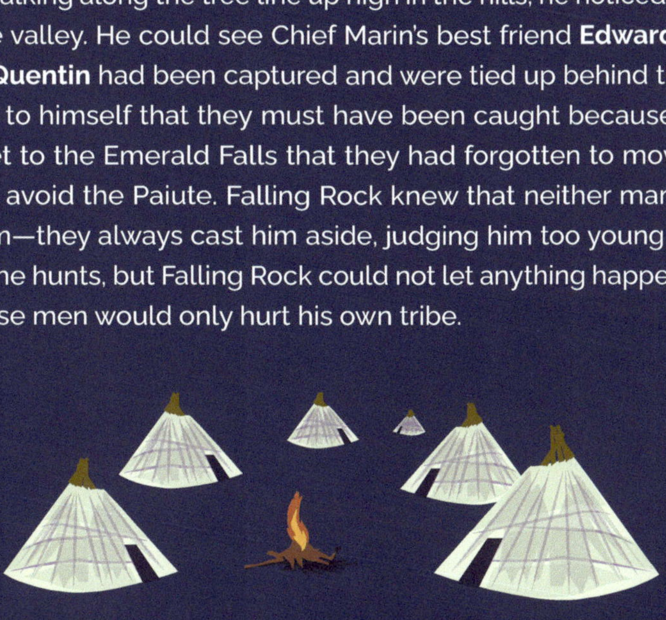

Falling Rock carefully made his way down the mountain, making sure not to be seen by the rival Paiutes. Quentin and Mr. Curtis were blindfolded and bound to an old redwood tree. Fortunately the Paiute were all gathering around their central fire to have their evening meeting. Falling Rock moved stealthy and with speed through the redwood trees, and with two swift cuts with his knife, he freed Quentin and Mr. Curtis.

Before Falling Rock ran back to the tree line, he spotted a medicine pouch hanging outside one of the Paiute huts. He knew that the Paiutes had herbs and medicine that the Miwok did not have access to—it would be a mistake to not bring it back to his village. Falling Rock crept up to the hut and snagged the pouch, then all three men raced into the trees.

The three decided to keep trekking towards the Emerald Falls through the night so as to avoid the Paiute. They made it to the Emerald Falls by daybreak. Then Quentin and Mr. Curtis pushed Falling Rock aside. They didn't believe that his young lungs and slimmer muscles would allow him to make it to the bottom of the pool beneath the falls to retrieve the Elecampane Root. The pool was deep and filled with dark, cold water, so dark that no light reached the bottom.

First Mr. Curtis dove in but quickly surfaced, choking and spitting water. The cold was so shocking that Mr. Curtis could not hold his breath. His muscles tensed, making it hard to swim. Next Quentin dove in from the far side of the pool, across from the falls. He was under the dark water for a very long time but when he emerged, he was empty handed and desperate for air.

While the older men caught their breath and warmed themselves in the sun, Falling Rock thought about Tamalpais, and how she was struggling for her life back at Huimen. Falling Rock then climbed to the top of the falls and studied the water. He noticed small air bubbles coming to the surface near the falls. He took a deep breath and dove off the falls into the cold, dark pool, letting the power of the waterfall push him down. Once the force of the waterfall had pushed him as deep as it could, he swam for a large rock with air bubbles.

You see, Stalking Wolf had taught Falling Rock about the Great Tortuga in the Lake in the Sky. The Great Tortuga was a turtle who lived beneath the falls and could swim deep under its water for hours. Falling Rock reached the shelf that the turtle hid under and latched onto its shell. Some people will say Falling Rock used telepathy to communicate with the turtle, but others will say he simply pulled on the turtle's tail to make him swim towards the bottom. He rode the Great Tortuga to the very bottom of the Lake and retrieved the root.

Once Falling Rock had the root tightly in his grasp, he pushed off the bottom and floated towards the surface. He barely made it without drowning. His body was so weak that he could not pull himself out of the water. Quentin and Mr. Curtis ran towards the frigid lake to pull Falling Rock's fatigued body from the muddy shores.

They propped him up against a tree. Falling Rock said, "Leave me here to rest. Build me a fire to warm my cold bones and take the Elecampane Root and this Paiute medicine pouch back to Tamalpais. When I am warm, I will travel back to Huimen."

Mr. Curtis and Quentin were shocked. They had just witnessed Falling Rock, the young lover, do what they could not. They agreed to his wishes and left to deliver the medicine to Tam.

They made it back to Chief Marin in five days and told the whole story of what happened at the Emerald Falls and the Great Lake in the Sky.

They explained how the water level was much higher than usual from the heavy rain that year, and how Falling Rock, thinking with his heart and feeling his love for Tam, was able to do what the other men could not.

But he had gotten compression sickness from diving so deep and coming up too fast. They said they had left him resting against a great oak tree with a fire so that he could heal before he made the journey home.

Falling Rock wanted Tam to know that he would always be her protector.

When a week had passed and there was no sign of Falling Rock, Chief Marin was concerned for his daughter's heart. He sent a group of his strongest warriors to go and search for Falling Rock. They found the great oak tree with a circle of ash at its base where he had rested before the fire lit by Mr. Curtis and Quentin. Falling Rock was nowhere to be found. They looked for days but discover no sign.

Over time, Tam's asthma improved with the help of the Elecampane Root that Falling Rock had retrieved. The seeds of the flower found in the Paiute medicine pouch were from Cannabis Indica buds and grew into a powerful herbal remedy for many illnesses, especially when combined with the indigenous Cannabis Sativa; both kinds of cannabis are still in use today.

But even though Tam physically recovered, she was never the same without her beloved Falling Rock. The Chief, too, was deeply saddened and upset with himself. Although he was happy that Tam was alive and well, his daughter's sadness left a hole in his heart forever. He did not give her hand in marriage to any of the men, since the true champion of the quest was Falling Rock, and he had never returned. If only Chief Marin had recognized the true love that had existed between Tam and Falling Rock from the start.

Tam's broken heart made her wiser, and the love she and Falling Rock had shared made her stronger. She grew into the mighty shaman and respected princess we talk about today, just as Falling Rock predicted.

Later in her life, word of her kindness and strong heart spread as far east as the Mississippi River to the Cherokee Native Americans who were cruelly pushed from their home towards the west on the **Trail of Tears.** Tam gave hope for the old ways to continue in a new land. In 1845, when she passed, the land on which she and Falling Rock were raised,

The Great Eye of the Turtle, was renamed Mount Tamalpais to honor her natural beauty and her ability to show kindness to all.

To redeem himself and find comfort with his own soul after Falling Rock's disappearance, Chief Marin wanted Falling Rock to be forever remembered. His wish was for Falling Rock's soul to live among the immortal great lovers for all eternity—not only in the night's heavenly sky, but on Mother Earth's land as well. The tribe still held onto hope that Falling Rock could be out there somewhere, so the chief had signs and monuments created across the land as reminders of Tam's hero.

Chief Marin's message lives on today. Whenever you're driving along a highway, you might notice the big, yellow signs that read, "Watch Out for Falling Rock...."

GLOSSARY

Cannabis Sativa A native plant used in North America by many Native American tribes to make medicines and rope. The plant was also sometimes used in peace pipe ceremonies.

Chief Marin A Coast Miwok of the Huimen tribe, baptized at around age 20 in 1801 at Mission San Francisco and noted as an *alcalde* at Mission San Rafael in the 1820's. He died on March 15, 1839. Marin County and the Marin Islands are named in his honor. He was the "great chief of the tribe *Licatiut,*" according to General Vallejo's semi-historical report to the first California State Legislature in 1850.

Coast Miwok The second largest group of Miwok, the indigenous people known as the Coast Miwok inhabited the general area of modern Marin County and southern Sonoma County in Northern California, from the Golden Gate north to Duncan's Point, and eastward to Sonoma Creek.

Edward S. Curtis A westerner and future sheriff, Curtis documented Native Americans, writing about the Miwok community's healthy competition. He was a "Friend of the Miwok."

Elecampane Root *Inula Helenium*, also called Horse-Heal or Elfdock, is a wide-spread plant species in the sunflower family *Asteraceae*. The root is used to make medicine. Elecampane treats lung diseases, including asthma, bronchitis, and whooping cough. It is also used to prevent coughing, especially coughing caused by tuberculosis, and to loosen phlegm so that it can be expectorated.

Fire Stoker The person in charge of heating the rocks for Sweat Lodge rituals.

Huimen Village A Marin county village of Coast Miwok and home of Chief Marin.

Lake in the Sky Lake Tahoe includes the Emerald Falls, one of the most photo-graphed spots in America's vast landscape.

Lovelock Was a settler stopped for wagons in Nevada, United States in the Hum-boldt River Basin, very near the end of the river. 20 miles outside the town is the Lovelock Cave, a horseshoe-shaped cave about 35 ft width and 150 ft length where the Northern Paiute Indians ancestors left a number of duck decoys and other artifact remains.

Mount Tamalpais A peak in Marin County, California, Mount Tamalpais is known locally as Mount Tam and often considered symbolic of Marin County. Much of Mount Tamalpais is protected within public lands, such as Mount Tamalpais State Park, the Marin Municipal Water District watershed, and National Park Service land.

Nephilim Loosely translated as, "giants." In the Hebrew Bible who are described as mysterious beings or people being large and strong. Some interpret them as hybrid sons of fallen angels (demigods). In Hebrew Nephilim literally means "the fallen ones."

Northern Paiute Indians A Numic hunter-gatherer tribal society, traditionally liv-ing in the Great Basin (eastern California, western Nevada, and southeast Oregon), the Northern Paiutes' pre-contact lifestyle was well-adapted to the harsh desert environment of their land. Each tribe or band occupied a specific territory, gener-ally centered on a lake or wetland that supplied fish and water.

Peace Pipe A ceremonial pipe used to seal a treaty or during important meetings. When Colonists came to America, they brought with them a type of hemp called *Cannabis Indica.* Both *Cannabis Sativa* and *Cannabis Indica* are known to have mind-altering properties.

Sub-Chief Quentin According to General Vallejo, Quentin was renowned as the Sub-Chief of Marin and skipper at Mission Dolores. in 1840, San Quentin Peninsula was reputedly named after him. San Quentin State Prison was added much later.

Sweat Lodge A hut, typically dome-shaped and made with natural materials, used by North American Indians for ritual steam baths as a means of purification. It is heated by hot rocks warmed in a fire outside of the hut.

Tomales Bay A long, narrow inlet of the Pacific Ocean in Marin County in northern California, Tomales Bay was heavily used by the Coast Miwok Native Americans. It is approximately fifteen miles long and averages nearly a mile wide, effectively separating the Point Reyes Peninsula from the mainland of Marin County. It is located approximately 30 miles northwest of San Francisco. The bay forms the eastern boundary of Point Reyes National Seashore. Tomales Bay is recognized for protection by the California Bays and Estuaries Policy. On its northern end, it opens out onto Bodega Bay, which shelters it from the direct current of the Pacific. The bay is formed along a submerged portion of the San Andreas Fault.

Trail of Tears In 1838 and 1839, as part of Andrew Jackson's Indian removal policy, the Cherokee nation was forced to give up its lands east of the Mississippi River and to migrate to an area in present-day Oklahoma. The Cherokee people called this journey the "Trail of Tears," because of its devastating effects on culture and human lives.

Year Without Summer In 1815, Mount Tambora erupted in Indonesia with severe global consequences. It wiped out a large segment of the world's population, and triggered strange weather and crop famine. In 1816, the spring after "the year without a summer," there was a huge, worldwide pollen bloom.

Yerba Buena Long used by Native Americans as a remedy for indigestion, colds, and even arthritic pain, Yerba Buena means "good herb."

Acknowledgments

I would like to thank the artist Eloy Bida
for adding his beautiful illustrations
to this project, and bringing color
to my words through his touching art.

About the Author

Based in Northern California, **Justin Kerson** is a healer
using mixed-media art as his tool to remind us
of our true self and all our potentiality.
Learn more at justinkerson.com

About the Illustrator

Eloy Bida is a Native Illustrator exploring indigenous
languages, pre-Columbian mythology, and Indigenous
music and arts. View more of his art at eloybida.com